Praise for *Mouth Like Burned Wood*

"...A beautiful collection that details and captures childhood in an enchanting and mesmerizing voice. It would be wrong to assume that the amount of pages requires little reading. These short stories and vignettes pack a punch. The words are carefully constructed and the characters naturally written, with meticulous detail paid to each scene. *Mouth Like Burned Wood* is poetry— beautiful and simple with a lyrical flow that remains throughout the collection."

—Natasha Persaud, Book Reviewer,
Vine Leaves Literary Journal

Mouth Like Burned Wood

two vignettes, two stories

Jan M. Leotti

Editing: Brittiany Koren/Written Dreams
Cover art design/layout: Ed Vincent
Cover photographs © Shutterstock.com
Category: Literary Fiction
ISBN: 978-0-9909483-1-5

Dedication

For Frazier Russell, whose delicate and sometimes brutal questions helped me discover what I wanted to say.

For my father. I miss you.
For my mother. Thank you for your strength.

Acknowledgements

Thanks again to the wonderful team at Written Dreams, Brittiany Koren and Eddie Vincent for their expertise.

Thanks to Jessica Bell, co-publishing editor/designer and Dawn Ius, co-publishing editor of *Vine Leaves Literary Journal*, *Peregrine*, the literary journal of Amherst Writers & Artists, and *Primavera* for taking a chance on me.

And with loving thanks to Paul. You are always there for me.

Vignettes

These pieces appeared in the first issue of Vine Leaves Literary Journal *in January, 2012.* "It Was Broken Accidentally" *was chosen for their collection,* The Best of Vine Leaves Literary Journal 2012.

Since its first publication, I've made slight revisions to "It Was Broken Accidentally."

Edge

We park in the same parking lot every year. There is always a space.

I hold Mother's arm and we lean forward as we progress up the hill.

My father is buried under the grass, surrounded by locust, pine, dogwood, and hemlock. He was born on Christmas Eve, kind of like The Lord. I don't visit his grave except in December, a ritual fused with Christmastime, ever since my seventh birthday. Like with church, I'm too busy to stop by the rest of the year.

Today snow is falling, and I like that. It makes me dream of ghosts. Berries have pocked the snow with red wounds. When I was a child, I dug graves for my small pets in the back yard: a lizard, a hamster, a bird. I imagined their blood draining into the soil, tree roots seeking out the blood, drinking it, and the leaves above rustling with new life. I'm scarred, I know. It's the curse of those touched by death. Our vision is forever binary.

I stare at the sparrows eating berries while Mother prays. I don't pray. Nature is my prayer. I'm like my father that way. He chose this spot. He was a seeker of beauty, and always told my mother: "When I die, bury me by your little, white church. It's heavenly there."

It's strange what I remember about him: the scent of pipe smoke, an engraved ship on an ivory bolo tie, the words "Give me a kissy."

I crouch and rub his tombstone clean with a ball of snow, brushing away fallen twigs and leaves. Mother finishes her prayer and we arrange the wreath at the head of the tombstone. Later, we will enjoy turkey and cranberries by the fire. The house will smell of burning wood, and the tree will twinkle with glass ornaments. When my sister arrives from New Jersey, laughter will ring throughout each room and wrapping paper will trail in the wake of my niece and nephew—

They never knew my father.

Mother and I hold hands. We are quiet. The red and green wreath gleams with false cheer. Sparrows flutter their wings, their black eyes watchful from the waving branches above. Snowflakes whirl past in a rush of wind. One brushes my cheek, a cold tear. The child who dreamed those morbid things so long ago is here. She wants to know if her father is in the bark of the hemlocks, in the clamoring branches of the dogwoods, or in the sighing pines. Is he a ghost? An angel? Or is he a snowflake falling from the heavens, delicate beauty balanced on a blade of grass?

It Was Broken Accidentally

Thunderclouds envelop the house, puffy and gray. My mother is standing by the French doors. I hide under her long skirt. Lightning blazes outside, and I cling to her leg. In the pulse of light, the roses in her skirt glow pink, and I breathe out. The clock strikes midnight and another flash turns the roses to skulls. It's dangerous out there. I wonder where my father's gone. Maybe he's on the road, rain under his wheels. I'm small and far away—I can't reach anything, not even the phone.

In an instant it's dark and the skulls morph into ghosts. I peer out from beneath my mother's skirt in time to witness the hands on the clock freeze into place. Time has stopped.

* * *

I imagine—

When I'm older and I leave my mother's house, I might want to find my way back—spread breadcrumbs like forgiveness.

"The birds will eat them," Mother says. She always sees the negative. But I'll do it anyway.

Before I leave my mother's house, I'll pack my childhood self in a box and leave it in the attic. When I return for the holidays, I'll find my family has unpacked it along with the flake board Santa. They'll hang Santa on the door.

At dinner, with jokes and jibes, their mouths full of turkey, my brothers and sisters will remind me how I was back then—frizzy-haired and pimply. Father will be silent, his face a tombstone at the head of the table. Will he approve if I grow up?

***

It's dangerous when it's stormy. Mother tucks me into bed. Thunder cracks the sky like a heart. I hide it under my pillow, the heart. It was broken accidentally.

Mother says, "Fairies know how to fix it. They'll sew it back together in the middle of the night."

I ask, "Why can't they come when I'm awake?"

She touches her own heart. "It's not their way."

When she leaves my room, I wait. My eyes are shut, but I'm not. I'll fool the fairies and catch them under a jar.

Hours pass. I open my eyes. I search the house to see if anything has changed. The fairies are tricksy—I don't apprehend them. It's dark, but the clock has resumed its *tap, tap, tap*.

My mother sleeps through the storm.

My siblings sleep through the storm.

My father is somewhere I can't reach.

***

In the morning, the sun breaks free—the windows are white with light. I reach under my pillow. The heart is whole. I run my fingertips over the stitching.

Mother told the truth. But there will be a scar.

Stories

*"The Prop" was first published in the 2000 issue of Peregrine, Volume XIX, Amherst Writers & Artists Press, Inc.

*"I Remember Like It Was Someone Else" was first published in the 2002 issue of Primavera, Volume 24/25.

The Prop

Before the curtain goes up, her father dresses her. He holds out lavender stockings, and she climbs into them, a cat's cradle, between his finger and thumb. He pulls them up, making sure the crotch fits snugly, making sure there are no wrinkles at her knees. He tugs a shirt over her head, twists her into a silver skirt, zipper at the back, his thumb pressing against the clip to lock it. He buffs her patent leather Mary Janes, shines the buckles, and warns her not to run or jump or move— "You'll scuff the shoes."

After her father changed, she spied him in the basement. Night after night, with hammer and chisel, he carved a pair of legs. He shaped the first thigh, then knee, curve of the calf muscle, ankle, heel, arch, and toes of the left leg, and with the same attention, he carved the right. He painted both of them the color of flesh and hung them from the rafters to dry. Afterward, he dressed them in tights and fitted them with small, black patent leather shoes.

The first time she climbed into the box, he told her there was plenty of room, and it indeed felt that way. But soon she realized there were her legs, and the thighs of the magic legs. There was the illusion of her body sliced in half, and there was her body— neck, breasts, arms, stomach, buttocks, sex, legs, and feet— whole, inside the box.

There was the saw, and at first she thought it was fake like the legs. But her father explained that it was real. He held it out for her, balancing it in his two smooth palms. He let her touch the teeth. He told her to be careful, but a droplet of blood had already bloomed on her finger.

He told her that during the act she should not speak or scream. She should not react to the saw, except to smile. She practices this by grinning into a mirror and pressing her fingernails into her thigh as hard a she can.

On the night of the show, she stands behind the curtain, very still. Her shoes and the shoes on the fake legs are polished. Her father is a good artist, and if it weren't for the warmth of her skin, the differences between the two pairs of legs would not be detected.

The curtain goes up revealing the spotlit box. The audience claps. She climbs in, pushes the fake legs out for the audience to see. Her father, the Great Margeaux, closes the lid.

Her hands are hot, and her fingernails grip the wood. Her legs are curled, soft underneath her silver skirt. She moves them, wriggling her toes inside her shoes. Splinters catch her stockings.

Haw, haw. Her father's saw begins. Keeping still now, she is keen for her part: to kick the fake legs when she is halved. Her smile is like a white knife. The audience gasps.

"Where's the blood? There should be blood," says a little boy in the front row.

Stupid kid, she thinks. *He should know the difference.*

Haw, haw. It's coming close. There is only a thin piece of plywood between her leg and the saw. She wants to break it, kick her live leg into the saw's path, teach the little boy a lesson.

Her heel is poised.

I Remember Like It
Was Someone Else

Dear

It started happening this past week. Like that, I start writing to my mother in my head—Dear Cicely Pierce. Sometimes, Dear Mom. Most of the time I just start rambling.

Last night it happened in my sleep. Out of nowhere I started speaking. When I woke up, my friend Gwen was sitting on the floor next to me, eyes squinting, arms folded, mouth like burned wood. "You left a note. She knows. What did you write?"

"I didn't write anything."

"Did you sign it?"

"I didn't write anything."

I haven't thought of her.

When Gwen leaves, I go into the bathroom, turn on the water, wait for steam. I step into the shower, roll the door closed. There's no window. Steam collects above my head, reminding me of the cotton we used to weave between the branches of our Christmas tree to make it look like it snowed. That was before my father died, when all we used to fake was snow.

Everything about me is medium. Medium brown hair. I used to want it blond like my mother's. I shut my eyes—they are hazel, mid-way between green and brown, while my mother's are green—and warm water runs down my face draining the cold from my eyelids and cheeks. I let the warmth run over my medium shoulders and medium hips. I shave my legs, watching the lather peel away like an old skin. In three months, I'm going to be sixteen and a half. I want to be born again.

I turn the hot on hotter, hoping it will pop me out.

You've got bad circulation like me, my mother said.

I keep turning the hot until there is so much steam I'm dizzy. I'm barely breathing.

Accident

When I was five, I flew through glass.
Diamonds everywhere.
I remember like it was someone else.

When I woke, my mother's cheek was nuzzling my mouth. I tasted my blood, her tears.

Alexia Rose, sweetie, sweetie—Doctor! She's awake!

I remember I couldn't run for weeks. Cast on my wrist, one on my leg. I got stitches under my eye, and they had to operate to take glass out of my head. The doctor said I was lucky—I would need only minor plastic surgery. I cried. I wanted a new face.

Even after they took the stitches out, the yellow under my eyes wouldn't go away. I never knew how bright a yellow skin could turn, like squash in places. I checked my face every day to see how much yellow had left. But all I could think was—that's my blood running away. Dead blood. Blood that no longer works.

When I hit the glass, my blood was red.

We'd just come from Robertson's. My new pink one piece clung to my body making my chest stick out. Look! Mom! I modeled for her, hands above my hips, thumbs pointing in toward my belly. LOOK! I said, dancing. I was dancing. I saw the back of her head. She was looking at my image in the window's reflection, I could tell. After my father died, she couldn't look at me, as if something in my face horrified her.

She was talking on the phone, holding it delicately between her shoulder and cheek, kissing its little sieve of a mouth. Look! I said. But she whispered to the phone, cradling it, smiling at it, stroking her long nail across its back. Then she waved at my reflection, and I thought she could see me. Watch! I said, and ran out of the kitchen.

There were diamonds everywhere.
I didn't think she'd ever come.
My blood, her tears.
When she leaned over me, her face was really close—her eyes—maybe not all green, her hair blond with dark roots, her onion breath in my nose.

Gwen

The wind was blowing, and my hair felt like needles on my neck. I was on the corner of High Street waiting for Gwen. I refused to watch TV while my mother snored. Since she'd been alone, she'd been drinking red wine, pouring it into herself like a transfusion. Still, before I left I took some, too, feeling new, tilted life pump within me.

Gwen was coming to pick me up. She was taking me to her boyfriend's apartment, where we were all planning to live. She was late.

Our block was quiet, all the houses lit with what looked like love. I hopped up onto the mailbox and buried my nose in Skullface's furry neck. He smelled like old sheets and earth. He was calm in my arms, purring, and I thought I could live on that and red wine for a while. The lesbians' house across the street was dark except for the TV. Its quivering light projected shadows against the window. I hugged Skullface and thought about when Gwen and me were in sixth grade. After my father died, I was afraid of the dark, and Gwen stayed over a lot. She slept next to me, her arm around my middle, our faces together. Her breath smelled like lime Sprees. I thought what it would be like to kiss Gwen, her mouth blushy and tight like a plum. It would make up for my unnoticeable mouth—the whole of hers crushing mine.

Once, when she stayed over, before we fell asleep, we hid under the covers and touched tongues. We screamed because it felt wet and slippery and a little rough. We brushed each other's hair and hugged each other like we were boyfriend and girlfriend.

We watched TV, and then she fell asleep, and I watched her eyelids flutter, and touched my fingers to them, wondering if I could read her mind.

A couple of times in the middle of the night we woke up and cut the satin roses off our undershirts—the tight, pink buds embarrassed us. We threw the roses at each other, laughed and screamed, but no one heard us.

Leaving

With burgundy lips I kissed the mirror, then outlined the wrinkled smudge with my lipstick, going over and over the same place, but each time a little further out. I wanted to see what it would be like to have a mouth people noticed.

I was drying my hair when Gwen left the message on the answering machine—"I'll be there in ten minutes. Be ready." The light blinked red. My digital clock clicked. The whole house clicked. The washing machine clicked through cycles. The dryer clicked off. The Swiss cuckoo clock clicked before chiming. A fly clicked against the window screen. My mother was at the mall.

I got up, but the big, burgundy lips stayed on the mirror. I wondered what would happen when my mother saw them. Would they look like some cryptic message? Would she think I'd been abducted?

As I walked to my closet, the plastic beads I'd hung over my canopy made a faint shattering sound. I'd found them in the trash, and thought they looked like Christmas lights, but they didn't light up, really. Only when the sun hit them. I took my fairy doll off the top shelf and jammed her into the top of my jeans. When I was little, I used to wish she'd come alive.

I packed another pair of shorts, and two more shirts. My knapsack bulged. My medium shoulders could carry it, though. EeeeAaaaw! I'm stubborn as a mule. Gwen would have to carry my books. I couldn't take them all, but I would take the poetry book my mother gave me before my father died. I never read any of the poems, but I liked the slipcase, shiny green, and scented. The angel on the cover had the white wings of a swan. Obviously, they were fake. But somehow, the painter made them look like they would work, like they could lift that angel into the sky, over the clouds, anywhere she wanted to go. Dillon Mead, Gwen's

21

boyfriend, said he had a crate I could use for a bookshelf. I'll paint it swan white.

Everything was packed. I teeter-tottered down the stairs past the china cabinet with its shouting crystal, through the kitchen that still stunk of eggs and a too ripe cantaloupe, and into the den where the butterfly decals on the glass doors had long ago chipped. I stood studying them. After my accident, my mother brought me in to see the decals—yellow, iridescent green, blue, magenta.

So you'll know where the glass is, she said, and sank onto the couch, palms mashing her eyes. So much blood, she said.

I opened the glass doors and stepped onto the deck. The pool glistened. I could hear the phone ringing from inside, but I didn't run to answer it. It wouldn't be Gwen, and if it was my mother, she would expect to leave a message on the machine—I stayed out with Gwen most days and nights. Anyway, my mother had told me it was time to grow up, that things just happened, that sometimes you found yourself out of yourself, that pain was your only true parent, and that when it spoke, you had to listen.

My knapsack pulled on my shoulder. It was hot, and the pool jets were whispering for me to jump in. I walked toward the back gate. Gwen would be here soon. I opened the latch and turned around. Staring at my mother's flowers, I said their names: balloon flowers, peonies, cone flowers, dahlias, black-eyed Susans, zinnias, foxgloves, bearded iris, impatiens, rose-of-Sharon, lobelia, yellow loosestrife, prim roses, sweet cicely.

Darkroom

Last week, Gwen got me a job at Jerry's Photo down the street. Jerry's got a huge stomach that twitches after he says, "I'm going out for an hour." Dillon accuses Gwen of making out with him in the darkroom.

I was hired to work the register, but sometimes I help out with developing. The darkroom air is red, and it makes my skin look bloody. After my accident my mother said, You've had more blood on the outside of your body than on the inside. When she was happy she'd rumple up my hair and say, Your scars look like zippers, my little zipper head.

My shift is from two to six, part-time for now. Gwen works ten to six. She does the same thing as me, register and darkroom. Most of the time she saves the darkroom work for me. She says she hates working like a mole. But I know my way around the darkroom— the precise temperature of the chemicals, the mechanical purr of the timer, the white pulse of the enlarger.

The past comes alive in here.

Next to the sink there is a small, light-tight closet for taking film out of the cartridge. Me and Gwen call it the coffin. I grab some film, shut myself into the coffin, and crack open the cartridges. In the dark, I feel for the edge of the film. I'm getting better at working in the dark, at knowing the distance between things, even though it takes me a while to wind all the film onto reels, place them into tanks, and cover them.

When I come out, I check the temperature of the developing chemicals, set the timer, and pour the sour smelling liquids into the tanks. In minutes, someone's life is in front of me. Suddenly there's a hand or a foot, a smile, a pair of eyes. Nine times out of ten it's a christening or a wedding or a birthday, and everybody's smiling. But I always look for the one in the background. The one who doesn't know the camera is on him, the one watching everyone else dance.

Where's that pretty smile, my mother had said after my father died, her eyes looking out the window.

Nine times out of ten they crop out the non-smiling guy.

One Great Thing

One great thing about Dillon Mead's apartment is I can see the whole room from my mattress. The door. The window. I've peered into the walls, seen their flimsy skeletons, rotting sheet rock, mouse droppings. I know them underneath. I've scraped them, scarred them, sanded them whole, painted them a white that isn't blinding.

One great thing about my place is Gwen and me are like real

sisters. We run down to the local deli, buy coffees and potato chips or spend all our money on Macadamia nuts. We sit on the curb and talk about how we're going to move away from Dillon. We go braless, and even though Gwen's bigger than me, I push my tits out for the passing boys. Sometimes they stop and talk to us, and for a while, we are swans.

One great thing about Dillon's apartment is watching the sun creep down the alleyway, through the window, and onto Gwen. It lights up her face, and I can see her clearly, drool glittering on her cheek. She sleeps with Dillon the way she used to sleep with me, eyelids fluttering, breath leaving her parted lips like a ghost. She sighs, and even though I can't read her mind, I understand.

I Remember

I remember our front lawn was always weedy. I used to take blades of crab grass and hold them between my thumbs and blow so they'd quiver and make a sound. I remember the sound was ugly.

I remember caterpillars with wide eyes. I remember Gwen told me the eyes were just markings and not real eyes. I remember the caterpillars' bodies were bright yellow and orange, and Gwen and me put them into a velvet jewelry box. I remember we crumpled up leaves for their food. The next day they were dead.

I remember snow. I remember snow. I remember snow.

I remember the headstone. It was shiny and hard. I remember my mother said she wouldn't let them carve the words *Here Lies* in it because she said Jason Pierce wasn't really in there, even though the mortician said they don't carve those words any more.

I remember the grave blanket in the snow.

I remember at Christmastime, my mother and me would go to my father's grave. We would search for a stick to hold down the wreath. I remember we would bring a hammer to pound the stick because the ground was no longer soft. I remember worrying that I would hit his heart.

I remember in spring, we would lift the blanket off, and there would be red shriveled berries in the mud.

Mother

What I remember about you is your mouth. You painted it bright red. Bright red against all those teeth. You hated that your smile was crooked. You hated pictures of yourself because you said you looked drunk, one side of your mouth flying up. Bright red. You said you weren't afraid. Even with your crooked smile you knew people couldn't resist you. Your green eyes, gold hair. Christmas colors. On the outside you strutted your stuff like you were the first lady—pink suits with eyelet lapels, navy jackets with brass buttons. White silk blouses. You charmed church parishioners, the pastor. The water meter guy, the pool guy, the guy who sold you fish, Jon at the card shop who sold you Lotto tickets—they all loved you.

It's five-fifteen and you've just pulled in the driveway. Your hair shines in the sun, a lion's mane, your skirt is wrinkled, but your lips are perfect red. You gaze at the ground as you walk up the back door steps. You barge through the kitchen door. You put water on for tea. You change your clothes—heels left near the nightstand, stockings draped over the chest at the foot of the bed, jacket and skirt hung, blouse and bra slung over the back of the rocker. You change into jogging pants, a sweatshirt, and slippers.

Earlier, I told you I wouldn't be home, that I'd be out with Gwen. You smiled and said, You're growing up so fast.

You pour a cup of tea.

I imagine you rocking on the edge of my bed, palms pressing your eyes, but who will clean the lipstick off the mirror? Your head will spin with crazy thoughts.

If you check the garbage can, you will find a note. Gwen thinks you are coming for us. She thinks I finished the note, but it's been five months. I'm thirty miles away, an hour by train, and you haven't come for me. Do you think I am dead?

25

If you check the garbage can, you will find a crumpled piece of paper. In my neatest script I wrote Dear. You will see how neat the letters are—you were always on me about my script. But if you check it, you will see how each letter is clear and straight where it should be, and curly at the loops—a flourish like you showed me. You liked things to look right. You will be proud. You will see how hard I tried.

Do you remember the time I ran into the back of the garage? It was a week after dad died. I was six. I was playing ring-a-levio and Gwen was it. I was running from her and I couldn't stop. I ran into the garage, palms out, and rusty nails pierced my hands.

When I saw you running from the house, your gold hair a fuzz around your head, mouth open, eyes wide, I was frightened. When you picked me up, your arm a wing around me, you said, Where's that pretty smile? and I smiled the brightest smile for you. And when you sat me down on the kitchen chair and cupped my hands in yours, I felt your blood, hot, underneath your skin. You dabbed my palms with cotton soaked in peroxide and it stung my skin alive.

Do you remember? That night you'd fallen asleep with the TV on. I stood over you, rubbed your back, felt you breathe that alcohol-breath that made you sleep. Your skin was smooth and white. You rolled over, and your mouth slowly opened, a dark taking shape like one of the photographs at Jerry's. You said, Alexia Rose, I'm cold, come sleep with me.

I got the blanket from the hallway closet and pulled it over us. You never opened your eyes, but looped your arm around me and kissed my hair.

In my neatest script I wrote, Dear—

Author's Note

When I began to study writing, it was the late 1990s. I worked in New York City as an assistant to an artists' agent, and my office, near Union Square, wasn't far from the school. Having plenty of time after hours, I would walk to class.

One December evening as I passed Union Square Park, I noticed an outdoor holiday bazaar had materialized overnight. Enchanted by an ornate vendor tent, I ducked inside. Smoky cinnamon incense flavored the air, and baskets tucked into every available space overflowed with red and green ornaments, spicy chocolate, and fine silk scarves embellished with partridges and pears. Gemstones glinted from gold and silver jewelry, and a myriad other trinkets beckoned with holiday magic. Tempted as I was to splurge, money was tight, and I bought something small—a silver half-moon ornament. I emerged from the tent and was struck by Christmas lights strung whimsically through the branches of trees. I breathed in the chilly air, holding the ghost of my breath for a moment. Snowflakes whirled passed me and I knew I was going to remember this night for the rest of my life. I would remember it because I knew I was straddling a doorway, one foot in the past, the other tentatively in the future.

I had no idea if I could write a short story, never mind a novel, but I was young. In my heart, I secreted the hope of one day publishing, having no idea how much work it would take. At the same time, I didn't understand how far into my soul this desire had crept. I was chasing something else back then—acceptance, I think. I didn't take it seriously, although suddenly, everything was fodder for a story. Every night on the train ride home from class new ideas sparked like logs on a winter fire, and I scribbled them down as fast as I could before their heat and light faded.

I didn't realize then that writing is a lifelong study. It takes years to perfect a voice and style. And so here I am, years later, remembering that night in Union Square Park, still practicing the craft of writing. I'm happily dedicated, determined, addicted, insane or all four. Whatever the case, I've been fortunate enough, while on this journey, to publish a few stories in literary journals, and have collected them here.

The first two are vignettes. A vignette, as applied to literature, is "a short literary sketch or description" (Webster's New World College Dictionary).

To me, these pieces seem as if they'd been written before the two short stories. They were not. They were written long after. But my experience, so far, is that a writer's most urgent themes appear early and stick around until some sort of cathartic satisfaction is attained. Then she moves on.

The second two pieces are full stories. "The Prop" is "flash fiction," while "I Remember Like It Was Someone Else" is longer, the first time I was able to write on a subject for more than two pages.

When I think back to that night in Union Square Park, I'm reminded how unsure I was about my ability to write, how committing to that future meant a leap of faith. I still don't know where this path will lead, but now, both my feet are firmly on it.

All of these pieces were initially published under my full name, Janîce Leotti or Janîce Leotti-Bachem. But regardless of what I call myself, I'm still me.

About the Author

Jan M. Leotti has published short stories in Peregrine, Primavera, and Vine Leaves Literary Journal. She wrote a ghost story called "The Headless Bartender" and her first novel titled *CLOSE TO DARK*. She rescued two cats, placed twenty-two orchids on her sunny front porch, and married an award-winning landscape painter named Paul Bachem. Jan lives with Paul in a sky-blue cottage in New York, where she eats enchanted mulberries every summer.

www.ingramcontent.com/pod-product-compliance
Lightning Source LLC
Chambersburg PA
CBHW050920120626
46552CB00004B/1675